PRESENTED BY

Alvin Son

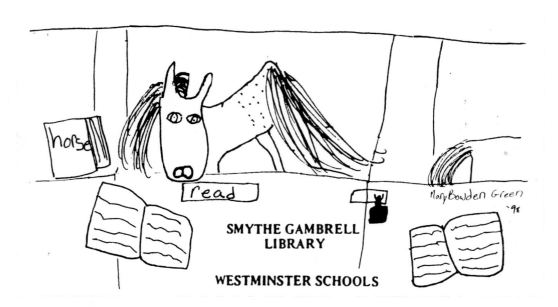

SMYTHE GAMBRELL
LIBRARY

WESTMINSTER SCHOOLS

Power and Glory

EMILY RODDA

ILLUSTRATED BY GEOFF KELLY

Greenwillow Books New York

Text copyright © 1994 by Emily Rodda
Illustrations copyright © 1994 by Geoff Kelly

First published in Australia in 1994 by Allen & Unwin Pty Ltd.
First published in the United States in 1996 by Greenwillow Books.

Printed in Singapore by Tien Wah Press
First Edition 10 9 8 7 6 5 4 3 2 1

Library of Congress Cataloging in Publication Data
Rodda, Emily.
Power and glory / by Emily Rodda ; pictures by Geoff Kelly.
p.   cm.
Summary: A boy wants to play with his exciting new
video game but keeps being interrupted by members
of his family who bring him back to reality.
ISBN 0-688-14214-1
(1. Video games—Fiction.)   I. Kelly, Geoff, ill.   II. Title.
PZ7.R5996Po   1996   (E)—dc20
95-1842   CIP   AC

For my boys. E.R.

For my girls. G.K.

For my birthday,

I get a video game:

POWER AND GLORY.

YES!

I put the game in my machine.  And play.

I walk the path.  I climb the wall.

I swim the stream. 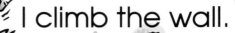 I find the key.

I search the cave. **I fight the witch…**

I fight the witch… I fight

the witch…

My **mother** yells:

"Breakfast!

Come to breakfast!

NOW!"

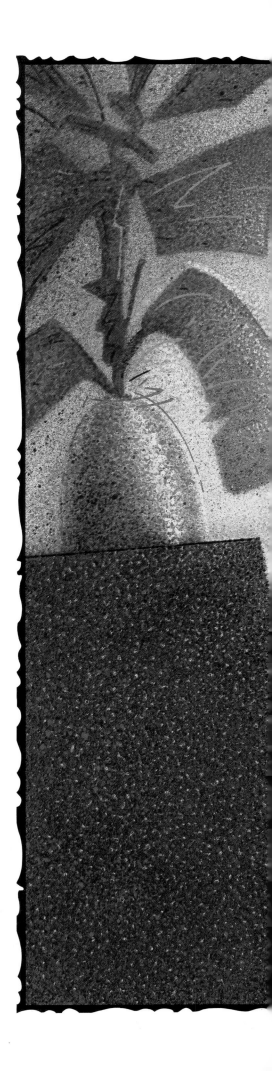

I put the game in my machine.  And play.

I walk the path. I climb the wall.

I swim the stream. I find the key.

I search the cave. I fight the witch.

I zap the witch. I run the cliff.

I jump the pit. The goblins charge...

The goblins charge... The goblins charge...

My **brothers** yell:

"A turn!

Give us a turn!

NOW!"

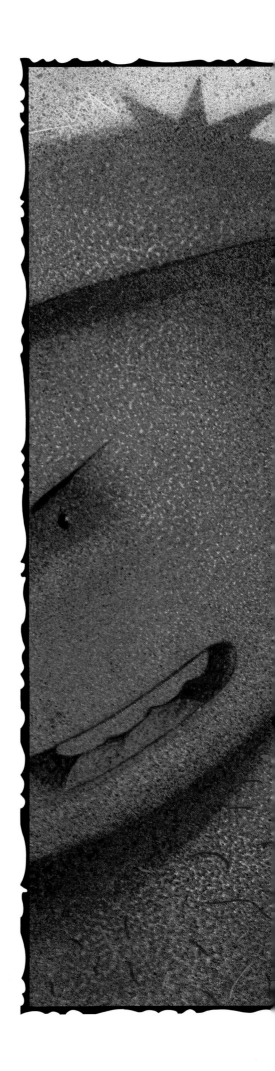

I put the game in my machine.  And play.

I walk the path. I climb the wall.

I swim the stream. I find the key.

I search the cave. I fight the witch.

I zap the witch. I run the cliff.

I jump the pit. The goblins charge.

The goblins fall. I catch the rope.

I ring the bell. The vulture swoops...

The vulture swoops... The vulture swoops...

My **sister** yells:

"My show!

I need to watch it!

NOW!"

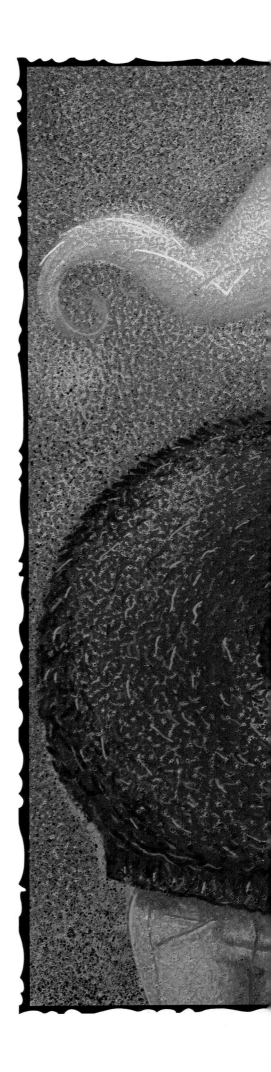

I put the game in my machine. And play.

I walk the path. I climb the wall.

I swim the stream. I find the key.

I search the cave. I fight the witch.

I zap the witch. I run the cliff.

I jump the pit. The goblins charge.

The goblins fall. I catch the rope.

I ring the bell. The vulture swoops.

The vulture dies. I swing to land.

I solve the maze. I face the beast...

I face the beast... I face the beast...

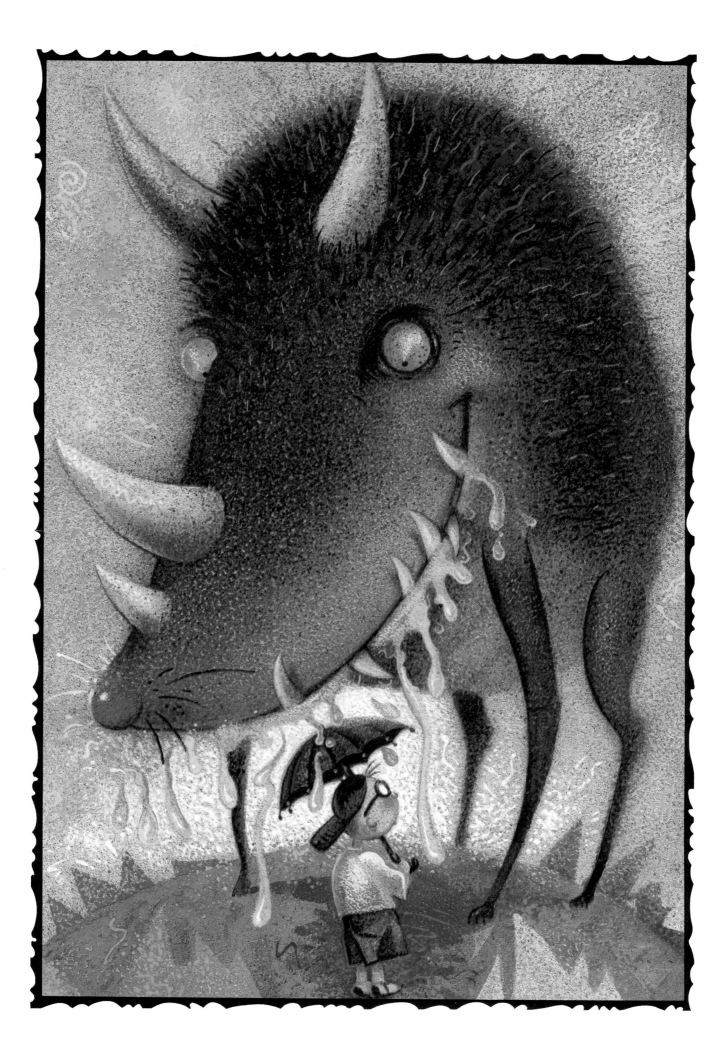

My **dog** barks:

"Walk! Walk! Walk!

Walk!

NO-O-W!"

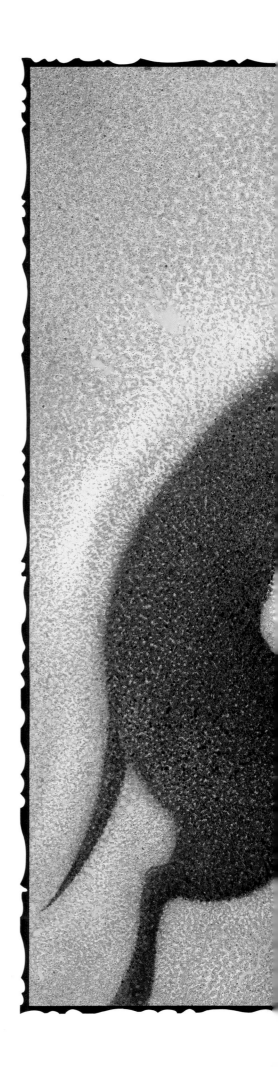

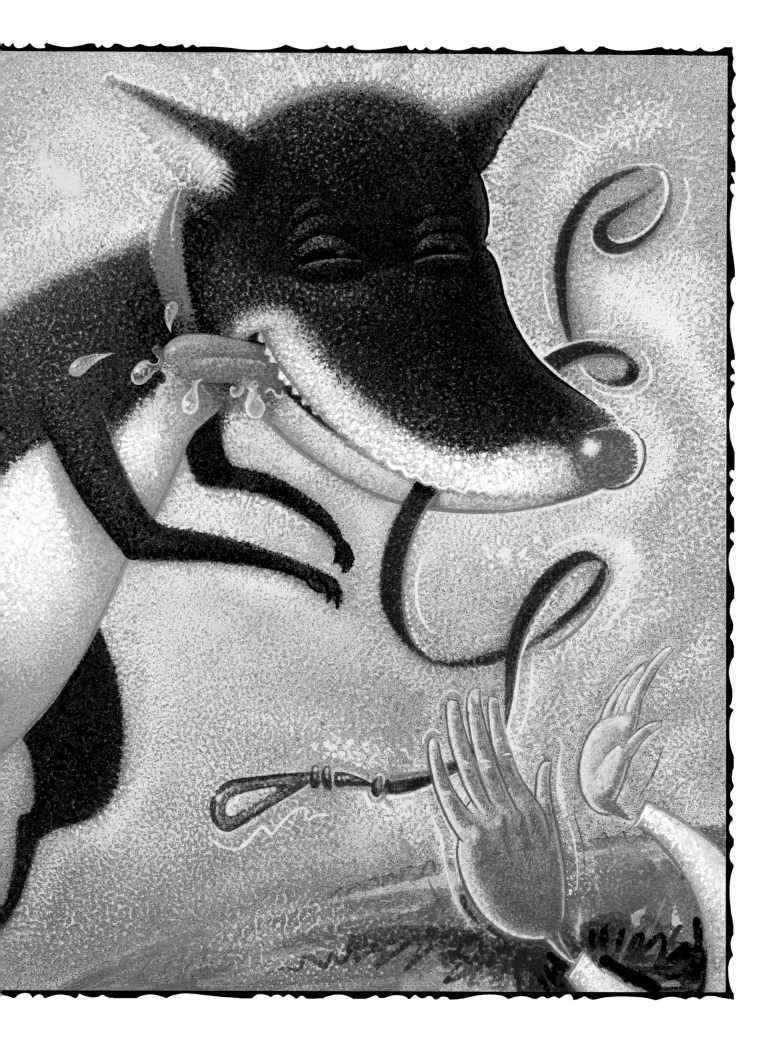

I put the game in my machine. And play.

I walk the path. I climb the wall.

I swim the stream. I find the key.

I search the cave. I fight the witch.

I zap the witch. I run the cliff.

I jump the pit. The goblins charge.

The goblins fall. I catch the rope.

I ring the bell. The vulture swoops.

The vulture dies. I swing to land.

I solve the maze. I face the beast.

I blast the beast. I leap the fire.

I grab the gold. The ogre comes…

The ogre comes… The ogre comes…

My **father** yells:

"Where are you all?

It's time to go!

NOW!"

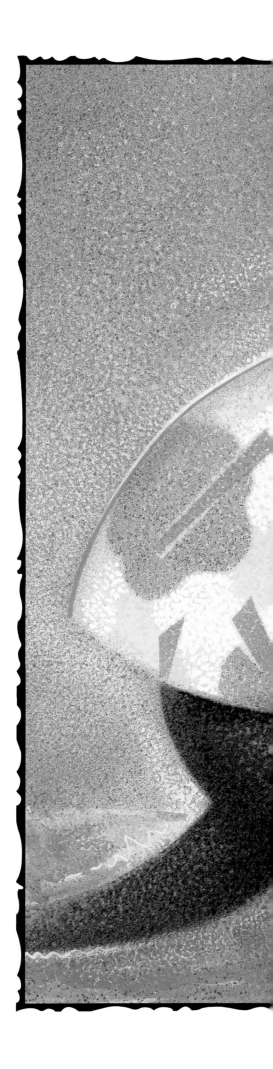

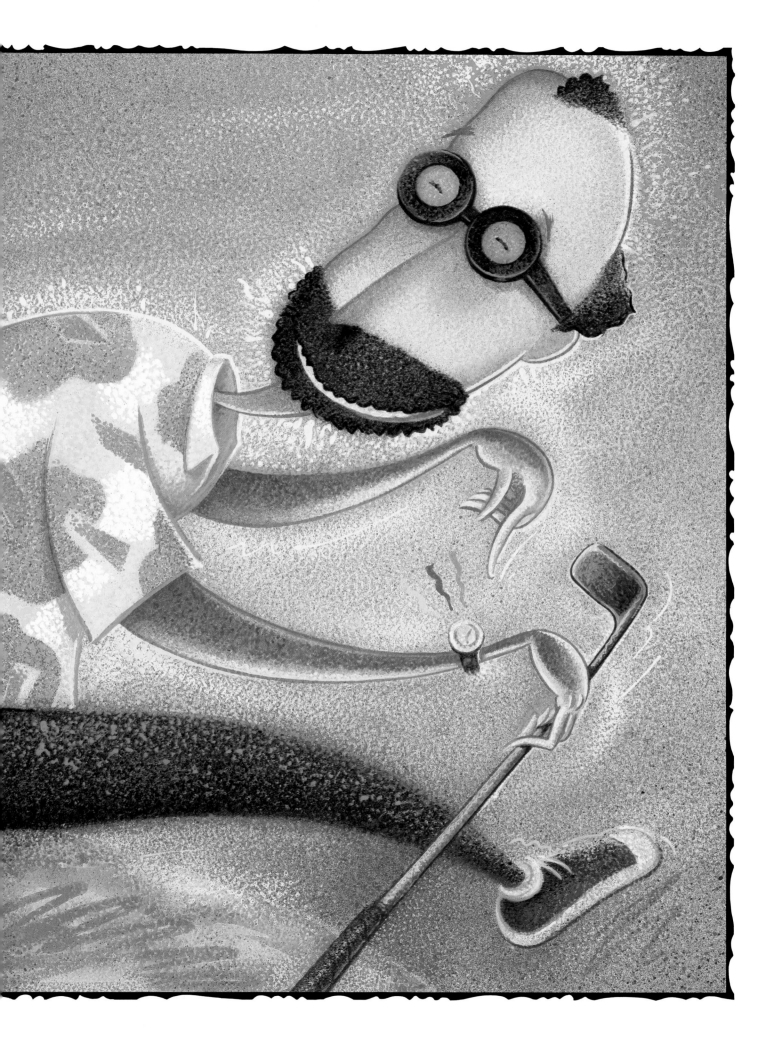

I put the game in my machine. And play.

I walk the path. I climb the wall.

I swim the stream. I find the key.

I search the cave. I fight the witch.

I zap the witch. I run the cliff.

I jump the pit. The goblins charge.

The goblins fall. I catch the rope.

I ring the bell. The vulture swoops.

The vulture dies. I swing to land.

I solve the maze. I face the beast.

I blast the beast. **I leap the fire.**

I grab the gold. **The ogre comes...**

The ogre comes...The ogre comes

And I

jump him,

thump him,

thrash him,

trash him,

mush him,

crush him,

I defeat him,

and I win!

YES!!!

Now for **level 2.**

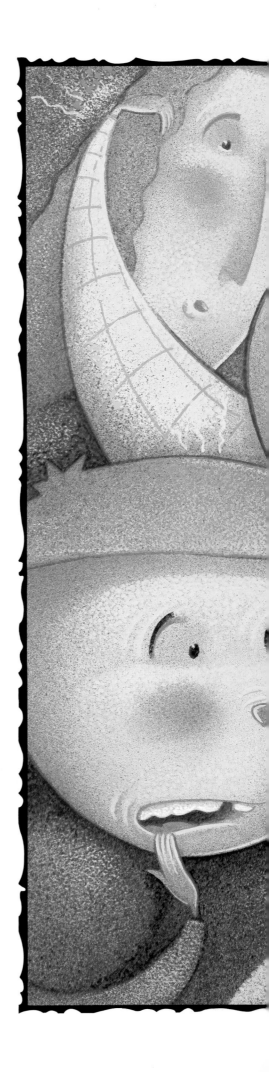

-The End-